SPEED SMASH

BY JONNY ZUCKER
ILLUSTRATED BY PAUL SAVAGE

Badger Publishing Limited
Suite G08, Business & Technology Centre
Bessemer Drive, Stevenage, Hertfordshire SG1 2DX
Telephone: 01438 791037   Fax: 01438 791036
www.badger-publishing.co.uk

Alien Speed Smash ISBN 978-1-84926-261-3

Text © Jonny Zucker 2010
Complete work © Badger Publishing Limited 2010

Badger Publishing would like to thank Jonny Zucker
for his help in putting this series together.

Publisher: David Jamieson
Editor: Danny Pearson
Design: Fiona Grant
Illustration: Paul Savage
Printed and bound in China through Colorcraft Ltd., Hong Kong

Contents

Badger Publishing

New words:

racer	announced
galaxy	frazzled
accelerator	draining
engine chassis	punishment

Main characters:

Jack Parker

Uggro Fristy

CHAPTER 1
Sprint Devil

It was Friday afternoon.

Tomorrow was the day of the
Inter-Galactic Youth Speed Race.

Drivers from all over the galaxy were
coming to Earth for the big event.

The human racer was a boy called Jack
Parker.

Jack had been driving since he was
seven. He was a very good driver.

People on Earth said he was going to win the race.

"Do not say that!" warned Jack. "There are lots of great drivers in the galaxy. It will be a very hard race."

Jack had a brand new car called Sprint Devil.

He was checking Sprint Devil's engine, beside the race track, when a very loud noise sounded behind him.

He looked round. A Creelon spaceship was landing in the middle of the race track.

The Creelons were hard and mean.

Out of the spaceship walked Uggro Fristy - the Creelon race driver. He was the same age as Jack.

Uggro walked over to Jack and took a look at Sprint Devil.

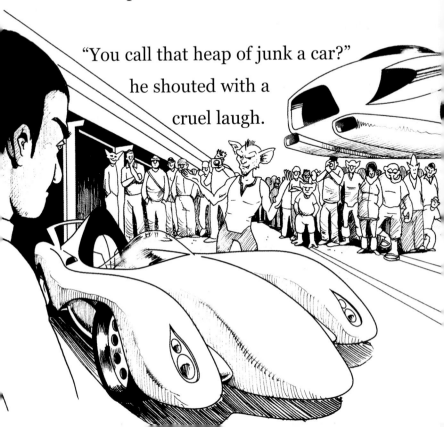

"You call that heap of junk a car?" he shouted with a cruel laugh.

"It's more than a car," replied Jack coolly. "It is the best car in the galaxy."

Uggro laughed again, even louder. "Yeah right!" he snapped.

"Well, where is your car?" asked Jack, looking at the Creelon space ship.

"You will have to wait 'til tomorrow to see it," said Uggro. "You will not stand a chance against me!"

"We'll see about that!" replied Jack.

As Uggro headed back to the Creelon space ship, Jack felt a twist of nerves in his body.

CHAPTER 2
What Was That?

The Sun was setting when the human tech team met Jack at the track.

"Take Sprint Devil for one last practice ride," said Adam, the boss of the tech team.

Jack climbed into the car and put on his helmet.

He powered the START button and Sprint Devil revved up. He pressed down hard on the accelerator pedal.

But instead of shooting forward, Sprint Devil spun wildly in a circle. Jack was shocked. He hit the STOP button.

The tyres screeched and the car crunched to a halt.

"WHAT WAS THAT?" he shouted, getting out of the car.

"Do not worry!" said Adam. "I think it is just a small problem with the steering. We will be able to fix it."

"Are you sure?" asked a worried looking Jack.

"Yes," smiled Adam. "Now go and get some sleep. The car will be perfect for you in the morning."

Jack woke up early on the day of the race. He ate breakfast and headed to the race track.

Lots of the other teams were already there. The Zambooli team were working on their thin and tall lime green car; the Gloops were testing out their very low silver and black oval-shaped car.

Jack hurried over to Sprint Devil.

"I was right," said Adam. "It was a tiny fault with the steering wheel. We have fixed it."

"So it won't happen again?" asked Jack.

Adam shook his head.

Just then there were cries everywhere. Jack spun round.

A huge yellow, red and black car was zig-zagging down the path beside the track.

Its engine chassis was massive. Uggro Fristy was sitting on top of the car, shouting at everyone.

"Take a look at the winning car!"
shouted Uggro. "We call her…The
Monster!"

Chapter 3

Starting Line

"Hey!" shouted Jack staring up at Uggro. "That car is too big for the race!"

"Oh yeah?" yelled Uggro, jumping down and coming face-to-face with Jack. "Let the judges decide!"

Three of the race judges walked over holding clip boards. They started checking out the Creelon car.

"Please be too big," Jack said under his breath.

The judges finished checking the car and whispered to each other.

The lead judge looked up. "The Creelon car is good to go," he announced.

Jack's face fell.

Uggro roared with laughter.

"Ignore Uggro," said Adam, making last minute checks on Sprint Devil. "You are a better driver than him."

"But his car is a monster," replied Jack nervously.

"Forget about his car. Just focus on the race!"

Jack took a deep breath. He lowered himself into Sprint Devil and checked all of the dials and buttons.

Everything looked ok. Adam and the human team pushed Sprint Devil to the starting line.

The Creelon team pushed The Monster right next to Sprint Devil.

"May the best car win!" grinned Uggro.

"I will see you at the finish," said Jack. "I will be there before you!"

"Dream on!" laughed Uggro.

The starter held his flag in the air.

Jack pulled down his helmet and the starter swept his flag downwards.

Jack hit the START button.

Sprint Devil did not spin round. It shot forward at great speed, with all of the other cars.

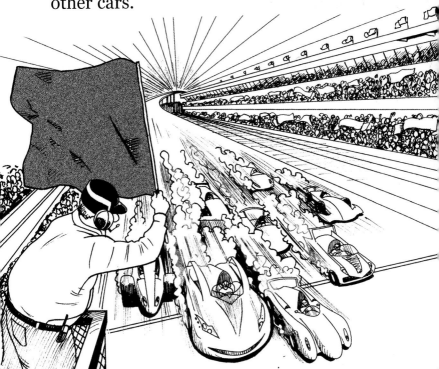

CHAPTER 4

Race Time

Jack took the first bend perfectly. He hit the straight.

He checked his mirror. The Monster was in fourth place. Jack sped on.

For the first two laps he stayed in first place. He was enjoying the race.

But near the end of lap three, he saw that The Monster was gaining on him.

As he swerved round the next bend, The Monster slammed into the side of Sprint Devil.

Jack and his car were smashed sideways. Sprint Devil was heading for a huge wall. The car was about to be smashed to pieces and so was Jack.

But Jack pulled down hard on the wheel. Sprint Devil skidded and spun and just missed smashing into the wall.

Jack slammed his foot down on the pedal and Sprint Devil leapt back onto the track.

The Monster was not that far away.

Jack was angry. There was no way he was going to let Uggro Fristy get away with nearly killing him!

I can catch Uggro and The Monster, he thought.

He crashed forward, faster and faster. He reached the side of The Monster.

Uggro saw Jack and laughed madly at him.

Jack flew round the last bend. The finish line was in sight.

Sprint Devil and The Monster were now side by side. Jack hit the pedal and Sprint Devil moved ahead.

The finish line was now less than a hundred metres away.

Jack moved further ahead.

He was going to win the race!

But with fifty metres to go, something terrible happened.

Sprint Devil began to lose power.

"WHAT'S GOING ON?" yelled Jack as The Monster overtook him and crashed over the finish line. Sprint Devil stopped thirty metres before the finish line.

All of the other cars zoomed past.

Jack had come last.

CHAPTER 5
Trophy

"WHAT HAPPENED?" yelled Adam running across the track.

"I have no idea!" replied Jack, climbing out of the car.

"Maybe you just took your foot off the pedal," said Adam.

"No way!" replied Jack. "Something is wrong with Sprint Devil. I know it!"

Adam and the human team checked Sprint Devil over. "There is nothing wrong with the car," said Adam.

Jack frowned. So what had gone wrong?

In despair, he walked over to the winners' area. Uggro and the Creelon team were posing for photos and holding up the silver trophy.

"Hey LOSER!" shouted Uggro. "What did I tell you?"

Adam walked over to The Monster. Lots of smoke was coming out of its engine chassis.

That's weird thought Adam; it should have cooled down by now.

He checked to see that no one was looking and flipped open the lid of the chassis.

He gasped in amazement.

Inside the chassis was a frazzled looking member of the Creelon tech team, with smoke coming off his body.

He was squashed in there with a mini laptop. On the screen it said, "POWER DRAINING" and listed all the other cars in the race.

Beside the words SPRINT DEVIL was a large red tick. It was the only car to have this sign next to it. They drained the power from Sprint Devil because Jack was about to win the race, realised Adam.

"I THINK THE JUDGES SHOULD SEE THIS!" shouted Adam.

A few seconds later, the race judges were looking at the over-heated

Creelon and his mini laptop.

"The Creelons cheated!" shouted one of the judges angrily. "They do NOT win the race. First place goes to Jack Parker and the human team!"

"YES!" shouted Jack, punching the air.

"NOOOOOO!" screamed Uggro running over to The Monster.

"Don't worry," said the Creelon in the chassis to Uggro. "There's always next year."

"No there's not," said one of the judges. "The Creelon team is banned for the next ten years."

"We better go home then," said the chassis Creelon.

"Not so fast," said the judge. "Your punishment for cheating is to clean up the entire stadium. But don't worry; it should not take you more than three days!"

Uggro put his hands on his head and groaned.

But Jack did not see any of this.

He was too busy holding the silver trophy in the air and grinning for the cameras.

RACING

Go-karting and racing are very popular sports for children and young adults. You can start racing in go-karts when you are eight or nine years old, but some children start as young as six.

Many Formula One drivers start their racing careers as child go-karters.

Formula One cars drive at incredible speeds of up to and over 250 miles per hour.

There are strict rules about the changes you can make to your cars. If you break any of these rules you get disqualified from the race.

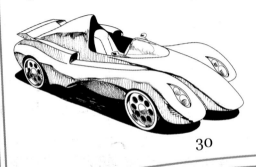

Most F1 cars are run by large companies with millions of pounds to spend on researching and making new cars.

Racing is a very dangerous sport and over the years many drivers have died. The most famous driver to have died is Ayrton Senna.

Sometimes Formula One drivers challenge drivers of 'normal' sports cars to a race. Nigel Mansell once raced against two very fast road cars. Even though he gave them a good head start, he beat them both.

To become a Formula One driver you need to spend lots of money. Many young drivers get a company to sponsor them.

Grand Prix races happen all over the world from Brazil to the UK. Thousands of fans flock to the circuits to watch the races live, while millions watch on TV.

QUESTIONS

- What noise alerted Jack when he was by the track checking out Sprint Devil?

- When did Uggro Fristy say that Jack would be able to see the Creelon car?

- What did Adam say the fault might be?

- How many other team cars are mentioned at the start of Chapter 3?

- What accident was Jack about to face?

- How far from the finish line did Sprint Devil lose power?

- How exactly did the Creelons cheat?

- What was the Creelons' punishment?